All Falling Down

Words by Gene Zion

HARPER & ROW, PUBLISHERS

falling down

Pictures by Margaret Bloy Graham

NEW YORK AND EVANSTON

ALL FALLING DOWN

Standard Book Number 06-026830-1 (Trade Edition)
Standard Book Number 06-026831-X (Harpercrest Edition)

to

N.F.

Petals fall from flowers
gently on the table

... gaily in the wind

Water falls

from the fountain into the pool

where little birds bathe and fishes swim

Apples fall down.

Children pick up the apples and put them in baskets

Sand castles by the sea fall down
    when big waves come rolling in . . .

The children build another one

Leaves fall down
Men rake up the leaves in little piles.

Nuts fall down. Squirrels gather the nuts they find

Snow falls down on the hills . . .
Boys and girls fall down in the snow. It's soft, it's fun

They fall on the ice. It's smooth, it's slippery

Snow falls down on heads and hats,
    on dogs, on cats who look out of windows,

on houses, on statues in the park . . . it's cold, it's white

Rain falls down.
It fills the brook and lake and sea.

It makes the flowers grow again!

Rain falls down on umbrellas and raincoats

as people hurry home

Shadows fall

getting longer and longer

Night falls

some stars fall down

Grandma's ball of wool falls down.
It's round, it's rolling.
The book falls down
    when Daddy's head begins to nod.

Jimmy's house of blocks falls down
and Mother says, "It's time for bed."
He slowly puts his toys away
then dreams until the morning when...

Daddy lifts him up and tosses him in the air.

He doesn't fall . . . Daddy catches him.